Henry Wowler
& the Mirror-Cat

Words by Rae Andrew
Artwork by Janet Flynn

Published by Herstory Writing & Interpretation
www.herstorywriting.com

First published in 2021 by Herstory Writing & Interpretation/York
Publishing Services
R.R.P. £6.99

ISBN 978-0-9928514-2-2

Printed by:
York Publishing Services,
64, Hallfield Road,
Layerthorpe,
York YO31 7ZQ
Telephone enquiries: 01904 431213
Email enquiries: enqs@yps-publishing.co.uk
Website: www.yps-publishing.co.uk
Order from: www.ypdbooks.com

Signed copies available direct from the author on her.story@hotmail.co.uk

CONTENTS

Chapter 1: Cat in the Hearth

Henry Wowler sat on the old sheepskin hearth rug, gazing into the fire. It wasn't lit. It wasn't even real. It was just a black metal grate, with shiny black glass at the back, and dull black plastic coals at the front.

He wasn't interested in the fire itself. No, he was watching the Other Cat, which he only ever saw at certain times and in certain places - like right here and now. With the same stripy ginger heads, long, stripy ginger tails, and ginger-splotched white bodies, they looked like identical twins - except that where Henry was soft, furry and warm, the Other was flat, hard and cold, with an odd, dusty smell quite unlike a cat.

Today it was there as usual, wide eyes staring back through the glass, copying his every move as he squished the fleece rug with his forepaws. Henry wondered if it was purring too, but as usual, he couldn't hear a sound. So imagine his surprise when the Other Cat suddenly spoke.

"Good morning."

"What?" gasped Henry Wowler. "Um- I mean, good morning. I, er, didn't realise you could talk."

The Other blinked. "What gave you that idea? I can talk as well as you can."

"Then why didn't you say something sooner?" Henry asked.

"I did, every time you spoke to me," it replied. "If you didn't hear, it's because you weren't listening properly."

Henry thought about this. "Well, I seem to be listening now. So tell me, please, who *are* you and what are you doing in my fireplace?"

The Other seemed to smile. "I could ask you the same question."

Henry puffed out his white chest. "I'm the Wowler - Henry Wowler – at home in my Third Favourite Sleep-spot, getting ready for a nap."

"Same here. And I'm the Mirror-cat. You can call me MC."

"Alright. Pleased to meet you, MC." Henry squinted through the glass. "Is it still night where you are? It looks pretty dark."

The Mirror-cat nodded. "It's always dark here."

"Oh?" Henry's ears pricked up. "That must make for good hunting. Do you get many mice on your side?"

"Oh yes, lots," said MC, "great big ones! Why don't you come through and have a look?"

"Me- how?" Standing on the coals, Henry touched noses with the Mirror-cat, then patted the glass with a paw. "I can't, I've already tried."

"But you haven't tried in the right way. Trust your whiskers, close your eyes, and don't open them again until I tell you."

Henry Wowler didn't like being told what to do. But he was so curious about the Other Side, and so keen to hunt lots of big mice in the dark, that he obeyed without making a fuss.

His whiskers quivered. For a moment, nothing happened. Then the fire-back seemed to dissolve. A chilly space opened in front of him, filled with the scent of well-fed tomcat. Then his nose collided with another, not glassy and hard now, but warm and alive like his own.

"There! It's easy when you know how." No longer muffled by the glass, MC's voice sounded loud and clear. "Now just follow me down - but remember to keep your eyes closed."

Eyes shut tight, Henry followed the Mirror-cat's nose through the fireplace, over the cold hearth tiles, and down onto a deep, fleecy rug.

"Well done!" said MC. "You can look now."

Henry did, and immediately noticed three things. Firstly, the light on the Other Side was very strange - not the luminous darkness of true night, but dull, flat and grey as if seen through tinted glass. Secondly, it all smelt very strongly of Mouse. And thirdly-

"Wow!" he gasped. "Either I've shrunk, or everything through here is big." He felt suddenly nervous. "*Very* big." He glanced at the Mirror-cat, the exact same size as himself. "Except you."

"Yes. But don't worry," said MC, "it's safe enough. Are you hungry?"

Henry nodded. It wasn't long since his breakfast, but he could always squeeze in a bit more.

"Right then," said MC, "let's go and eat!"

Henry slunk after him, past a skirting board that towered over their heads. He sniffed. Through the strong mousy scent, he could smell

something else – something tasty. Then, tucked into the corner, he saw a strange object - a wooden board, longer and wider than he was, with metal bars at one end attached to a spring in the middle. Beside the spring was a round brown thing on a metal plate. It smelt like a cat-biscuit, the sort he ate every day by the handful – but this one was the size of his head and looked as if it could feed him for a week.

"Wow! That's the biggest biscuit I've ever seen!" Licking his lips, Henry rushed eagerly forward.

"S-stop!" hissed MC, pulling him up by the tail. "It's a trap. Stay back, I'll show you." Crouching low, he carefully stretched out a paw and gave the biscuit a poke.

Swish-WHACK! A bar whizzed over and smacked down hard on the board - just as it would've smacked down hard on Henry Wowler, if he'd been standing there.

"Ugh." Henry shuddered. "I thought you said it was safe here!"

"It is… more or less. And *this* thing's safe now. See?" MC crunched into the biscuit. "Yum! Come and tuck in."

Very cautiously, Henry Wowler stepped aboard. Nothing nasty happened, so he crouched beside MC and started to munch.

"Mm-num-num-num," he purred. "Very good."

The two cats ate until their furry white bellies bulged fat and round like dandelion clocks. Then as they sat washing their faces, they heard a sound in the next room. It was a sound Henry Wowler had heard many times before – a scurrying, scratchy sort of sound – although never as loudly as this.

"What's that noise?" he said. "Is it a-"

"Oh, yes! Come on," MC headed for a huge doorway, "it's time for some fun."

Henry followed the Mirror-cat through into the huge kitchen beyond. Then he froze. As expected, he saw a mouse – but not the sort he was used to. Snow-white, with a pink nose and ears, and a white frilly apron tied round her middle, she was bustling about on her hind legs, sweeping the floor with a broom clutched in her forepaws. By local Mouse standards, she was a pretty, dainty little thing - but to the cats, she was simply Enormous.

"Watch this," whispered MC.

As the mouse-wife scurried past, he darted out, chased her long tail and nipped the tip with his teeth.

"Eek!" she squeaked. "What's that?" Looking down, she saw MC hanging on the end of her tail. "EEK!" she squeaked again, louder.

Shaking off the tiny cat, she jumped onto a stool, whipped up her tail and curled it round herself. Then she spotted Henry Wowler, and her big pink eyes almost bulged out of her head.

"EEEEK!" she squeaked, at the top of her voice. "Maxi! Maxi Mus! Help me!"

"What is it?" An even bigger grey mouse scurried in. "What's wrong, Mini dear?"

"Cats again!" She pointed a trembling paw. "Two of them, this time! Oh, catch them! Kill them! Get the horrid little things out of my house!"

"Don't worry, my love." Mr Mus took her sweeping brush and pushed the back door ajar. "I'll soon get rid of them."

MC winked at Henry. "Get ready to run," he hissed.

Swish-WHACK! Maxi's broom thwacked down on the floor, just missing their tails, as the cats bolted for the door. "You frightened my Mini!" he cried, chasing them out. "I'll squash you flat, you little pests!" Swish-WHACK! He brought the broom down again.

The cats fled into a garden the size of a football field and hid behind a huge plant-pot while Mr Mus searched around, muttering threats and gripping his broom in a menacing way.

"When you said- the mice here were big- I didn't think you meant- *this* big," panted Henry. "And it doesn't seem very safe at all!"

"Oh, Maxi's alright," said MC. "He misses on purpose. Watch this." He popped out from behind the plant-pot and said, "Miaow."

"Aha! There you are, you little rascal," said Maxi. Stooping, he held out a paw.

Henry was amazed to see the Mirror-cat jump onto it. "Come on, Henry!" he called. "Maxi won't hurt you, I promise."

Slowly, fearfully, Henry Wowler crept out from hiding.

"Aha! And there's your little friend! Here, kitty-catty," said Maxi.

Slowly, fearfully, Henry crept up and huddled beside MC.

"Well, well." The mouse inspected them closely with his beady black eyes. "Just look at you two! Alike as two peas in a pod."

Henry couldn't help cringing as a huge claw approached. Then it scratched the back of his head, very gently, and he couldn't help purring.

"Aw," said Maxi. He petted MC, too. "Sweet little kitties. But you're very naughty little kitties too, for tormenting my poor missus! So run off and play somewhere else for a while." Very gently, he lowered them to the ground. "And don't let her see you come back in – or maybe next time I *will* squash you flat!"

Winking one great eye, Maxi Mus scurried off with his broom, shouting, "Here, kitty-catties! Come out and let me whack you!"

"Told you so." MC trotted off with his tail in the air. "Now follow me," he said over his shoulder. "There's something I really must show you."

Henry Wowler wasn't sure he wanted to see whatever it was. But he didn't want to be left alone either, so he trotted quickly after MC down the long garden path.

After what seemed like miles, they came to a huge wooden gate with plenty of room for two tiny cats to sneak underneath. Outside, Henry saw a street exactly like his own, but ten times- no, a *hundred* times bigger! And sure enough, there were lots of great big mice - scuttling home with nuts and seeds for dinner, out in their gardens picking berries and bedstraw or standing around squeaking gossip with the neighbours.

MC nudged Henry. "Look over there."

Henry looked. At the end of the street he saw a grassy playground, where dozens of mouse-children were dashing through tunnels and mazes and racing around inside revolving wheels. Even the infants were far too big for them to hunt; still, the sight of the young rodents playing made the cats' paws itch and their tails lash back and forth. So they couldn't help slinking further out onto the pavement to get a better view - and were much too busy watching to notice what was creeping up behind them.

Suddenly, Henry Wowler felt himself caught by his long ginger tail. A moment later he found himself dangling helpless in mid-air, yowling in pain and shock. Then he was set down on a big pink paw, with his tail still firmly gripped.

Two high-pitched voices squeaked together. "Gotcha!"

Henry crouched, frozen with terror. His eyes, darting round frantically, saw MC caught in the same way and looking just as scared.

Their captors were two boy-mice, wearing caps on their heads and school scarves round their necks. "Ee!" squeaked one, as they compared their catches. "Orange and whites! How pretty! A matching pair, too."

"Yes," squeaked the other, "let's take them home and put them to live with the rest!"

"We can't, we'll be late for school. Mummy wouldn't let us keep them, anyway," sighed the first. "She says we've got too many kitties already. No, let's take them with us! I bet Miss Skeech won't mind. She can put them in the cage with the other class pets."

In a cage? Henry didn't like the sound of that at all. Desperate to get free, he sank his teeth into the paw and kicked at it with his hind-claws as hard as he could, while MC did the same to the paw holding him.

"Eek!" squealed the boy-mice. "I'm bitten! I'm scratched!"

Shaking their sore paws, they dropped the cats – who landed on all four feet and, quick as a flash, darted back under the gate, back down the garden path, and dived around the corner of the house out of sight.

"Phew!" panted MC. "That was a lucky escape!"

"Yes," panted Henry Wowler. "And I don't want any more, thank you very much! I want to go home now. I don't like this place. No offence," he added hastily, in case it sounded rude.

"None taken," said MC. "Follow me, then, and mind Mrs Mus doesn't see you."

There was no danger of that. Mini was still far too busy scolding Maxi, who had kindly left the door open a crack, about his useless cat-traps, uselessness as a cat-hunter, and general failings as a mouse-husband, to notice them creep back in. (He saw them though, and he gave them a knowing look as they slunk silently along the kitchen skirting board, back to the living-room and onto the fleecy rug).

"Well," said Henry, "thanks for showing me around. It's been very-um, different."

"You're welcome," MC replied. "Goodbye, Henry Wowler. I'm sure we'll see each other again soon."

He touched his nose to Henry's. "Now," he pushed gently, "shut your eyes and back into the fireplace."

Henry obeyed, awkwardly, nose to nose with MC. As his hind-paws, then his forepaws, scrabbled over the tiles and fake coals, the Mirror-cat's voice grew muffled and faint. "That's right… keep going… nearly there…" The pressure on his nose became chilly and hard… then disappeared altogether.

Henry Wowler opened his eyes. He blinked in surprise. He wasn't standing with his head and front paws in the fireplace, as he'd expected. Instead, he found himself curled snugly in his Third Favourite Sleep-spot on the hearth rug. Surely his adventures on the Other Side hadn't been only a dream? He stood, yawned, stretched, and turned round three times, considering. Then before returning to his catnap, he glanced into the fire.

The Mirror-cat caught his eye and winked. Henry winked back. He lay down again on the fleece and washed his tummy, which was still bulging with biscuit. Then he put his head on his paws and closed his eyes with a sigh of contentment.

No, he decided as he drifted off to sleep. I don't think I dreamt it. I think it really, truly happened...

Chapter 2: Cat in the Wardrobe

Flat on his belly, Henry Wowler slunk into the bedroom. Slowly and silently, he crept over to the wardrobe and squinted up. The mirror on the door showed only the foot of the bed and the opposite wall.

So far, so good! Very slowly, he raised his head. Very slowly, two big ginger ears rose into view, then a stripy ginger forehead and two greenish-gold eyes.

Yes – no matter how hard he tried to catch MC out, somehow his friend was always ready on the Other Side, waiting for exactly the right moment to appear. The two cats touched noses. They stood on their hind legs and scrabbled at each other with their forepaws, pink pads squeaking on the glass. Leaping apart, they humped up their backs and fuzzed out their tails. Then they danced back together and started to box, trying hard to clip each other's ears. As usual, neither could win; so at last they gave up and sat, face to face.

"Hello, Henry," said the Mirror-cat. "How are you today?"

Henry yawned. "Bored now."

"Me too! You should come through and play."

Henry hesitated. "With great big mice? Um, no thanks."

"No, no, there aren't any here – and we'll have fun, I promise! So come on, you know you want to. Do you remember how?"

"I think so." Henry stood up, shut his eyes, and pressed his nose to the glass. Whiskers twitching, he waited. When MC's nose grew warm against his, he took a slow step forward, then another and another; and when his whiskers sensed the Other Side air all around, he opened his eyes.

This room didn't look any bigger. If anything, it looked smaller… and that, he realised to his great surprise, was because *he* was bigger, standing tall on two legs. The Mirror-cat stood beside him, also on two legs, and wearing a neat little white shirt, a red stripy tie, and a pair of grey shorts.

Henry looked down at himself. His jaw dropped. He gasped. "What? How? Why have we got Ooman clothes on?"

"That's just the way it is here." MC bared his teeth in a strange grin. "Different mirrors show different reflections, you know."

"Well, I feel silly like this." Squirming his neck, Henry pawed at his tie. "Not to mention uncomfortable."

"Don't mention it, then!" said MC. "Don't even think about it. Come with me, I'll show you something to take your mind off it."

Trying very hard not to think, Henry followed MC down the landing. Sure enough, after a few steps it seemed quite normal to be walking on his back legs, and he quite forgot that he was wearing clothes.

The Mirror-cat opened a door. "This is my room."

"You have a whole room of your own? Wow." Envious, Henry looked in. It had blue-and-white tiger-stripe wallpaper, a blue carpet, blue curtains, and a blue fluffy blanket on the snug little bed. There was a toy-box filled with stuffed animals, jingle-balls, and catnip mice, a desk and chair in the corner under a shelf full of books, and a chest of drawers facing the window. Standing on top of this was a large wooden hutch, shaped like a three-storey house, with bars on the front.

MC whispered, "These are my pets. Come and look," he beckoned, "but don't make a noise or any sudden movements. And most of all, *don't* claw at the bars - it really upsets them."

Very curious, Henry Wowler peered into a triangular room at the top, beneath the pointed roof. The narrow space where the sloping walls met the floor was stuffed with matchboxes and bottle tops, piles of shed claws and whiskers and cat-fur, and bundles of twigs and dried grass; and arranged along the back wall, odd items he didn't recognize. But there was no sign of any living creature, so he peeped into the two rooms below. The one on the left had a grey mouse-skin rug on the floor, and a bean-bag bed covered with blankets of felted white cat-fur. The one on the right contained a white rubber tub next to a round white pot with a wooden lid. But nothing was sleeping on the bed, and nothing was bathing in the tub, although it still held traces of water, and small squares of damp cloth were hanging to dry on a dowelling wall-rack.

So Henry looked in the single large room at the bottom, which was carpeted all over in brown rabbit-fur, and had delicate hangings in rust, grey and white covering the walls. One end was furnished with a dining table and two chairs made of pale varnished wood, and a matching dresser arrayed with little china cups and plates. At the other end was a brown beanbag couch and two armchairs arranged round a low wooden table, and there, at last, Henry saw MC's pets sitting still and quiet: a black-haired male, a golden-haired female and, nestled by their feet in a tiny white basket, a tiny pink bald infant.

"Wow!" he gasped. "Are they *real*? And alive? Real live Oomans? But how can they be? They're so small!"

"Shush," hissed MC, "you'll wake the baby! Yes, Oomans *are* small here. Different mirrors show different reflections, remember?"

Henry waved at the pair. They waved back. "Aw – they're really sweet! Have they got names?"

"Yes, we call them the Bright Family because they're so clever. He's Benjamin and she's Tabitha – Benji and Tabbi for short - and they've named the baby Kit, but we're not sure yet if it's a boy or a girl.

'And they get up to all sorts of tricks. I often fetch them stuff just to see what they'll do with it." MC pulled a shiny blue-black feather from his pocket. "I picked this up on my way home from school. I think it's a magpie tail-feather. Watch, now!"

He held it front of the hutch. Tabbi Bright clapped her little hands, while Benji Bright jumped to his feet, making a high-pitched chittering

18

noise. Then he dashed over to a ladder in the corner, scrambled up into the bedroom, dashed through the bathroom, and scrambled up a second ladder to emerge into his attic workshop.

MC poked the feather through the bars. Benji grabbed it, chittered his thanks, then sat down on the floor and began plucking black strands off the stiff central quill, and laying them in the nearest empty matchbox.

Puzzled, Henry asked, "Why's he doing that?"

"For Tabbi to spin into thread then weave into cloth. See those things at the back? That's her loom and spinning wheel." MC pointed them out, standing by the wall surrounded by baskets of fur and feather strands waiting to be spun into yarn. "She made all their blankets, and some of their clothes, and those wall-hangings in the bottom room. And Benji uses the quills to weave the little baskets, although he made the baby's cradle from Papa's old whiskers."

"Wow," said Henry, impressed. "If they can do all that, they must be bright enough to open this hutch! Do they often escape?"

MC shook his head. "Oh, no, Oomans are very affectionate and loyal when they're properly cared for. And that's not hard to do – they're really easy to house-train, and they mostly look after themselves.

'Look - Tabbi does all her own washing and cleaning." He opened the top drawer of the chest to show Henry her little buckets and bowls, sponges and cloths, cakes of soap, tub and washboard, small straw broom, a duster made from a bunch of short feathers tied to a twig, a round white pot with a wooden lid, and a small roll of white tissue-paper.

"All I have to do is empty and wash their potty every day." MC unfastened the hutch, took the used pot from the bathroom, replaced it with the clean one from the drawer, and added some fresh squares of tissue. "Apart from that, I just give them water, hot and cold, every morning and night, and take them outside at least once a day for an airing. Oh, and deliver their food, of course, but they make their own meals – *and* do their own washing up."

"Wow," repeated Henry. "What do you feed them on?"

"Whatever Mama feeds me and Papa. But Oomans need plants to eat as well, so we've made a special plot in the garden, with an outdoor hutch for them, and we grow fruit and herbs. I pick some fresh every morning before school. Sometimes they come with me and help."

19

Henry grimaced. "Keeping Oomans sounds like hard work."

"I don't think so," said MC. "Besides, they're good company - Tabbi and Mama do needlework together, and Benji and I build furniture." He opened another drawer containing paintbrushes, tins of paint and varnish, modelling knives, tubes of glue, dowelling rods, fabric remnants and stuffing. "Papa helped us finish the dining room dresser last week, and next we're going to refurnish their bedroom. So I'm doing extra chores to earn extra pocket money, because that kit's expensive – it comes with a feather mattress and pillows, all the bedding, and a wardrobe, and a dressing-table with a stool and real mirrors! And when *that's* finished, the whole hutch will be properly furnished."

It struck Henry Wowler, whose own hobbies included bird-watching, chasing mice, and looking out of the window, that MC's pastimes were extremely unusual for a young cat; and he was about to say as much when another voice spoke behind him.

"Have you finished tidying your room, son?"

Henry turned round and got the shock of his life. Standing by the door was a beautiful lady-cat with long, perfectly groomed peachy fur – a lady-cat he hadn't seen for years and had *never* seen wearing a pearl collar and a dress of the same emerald green as her eyes. Still, he recognised her in a flash and squeaked like a new-born kitten. "Mama!"

The lady-cat seemed not to hear. "Ah, yes. Nice and neat." She patted MC's head. "Now, be an extra-special boy and pop round to Mewly's for a box of Papa's biscuits, we've run out." She gave him a coin. "If you get back before he does, you can keep the change."

"Ooh! Thanks, Mama!" cried MC, dashing out of the room.

Henry Wowler dashed after him, downstairs, out through the front

20

door, down the garden path and, with a flying leap over the gate, onto the pavement beyond.

"This way!" MC grabbed his paw. "Hurry up!"

They trotted off down a street exactly like Henry's own - except that everybody on it was a cat. There was a post-cat, delivering mail from a red sack on his shoulder, and a black coal-cat delivering fuel. A tabby housecat with a shopping bag was mewing over her neighbour's pram full of fluffy new kittens, and on the grassy playground, a big gang of school-kits was having fun chasing balls and climbing trees.

"Wow!" Henry dug his hind claws in. "Can we stop to play?"

"No time." MC dragged him on. "Papa will be disappointed if he can't have his favourite biscuits with his milk when he gets in from work."

"Work?" Henry blinked. "Your Papa *works*?"

"Yes, he's Head of Feline Resources for Catchester Council," MC said proudly.

Henry Wowler had no idea what that meant. But it sounded much more important than what his own father did - lazing in the sun, chasing lady-cats, and fighting other tomcats.

"And Mama's a housecat and part-time fur-dresser," MC went on, "and I'm trying hard at school because I want to pass my exams so I can get a nice job working with Oomans when I grow up. What are *you* going to do, Henry Wowler?"

"Er- I haven't thought," confessed Henry. Then he suddenly noticed how far they'd come - all the way up the hill and round the bend, almost as far as the row of shops on the corner of the main road - much further than he'd ever dared venture before. He clasped MC's paw tight, suddenly feeling very small and helpless, and a very, very long way from home.

"Don't worry." The Mirror-cat seemed to read his mind. "Just look around. There's nothing here to hurt us."

Nervously, Henry looked. Sure enough, there were no dangerous dogs on the loose - no dogs at all, in fact, except for a docile Great Dane pulling the coal-cat's delivery cart. There were no dangerous Oomans, only a pair of youngsters naughtily tangling their leads while their lady-cat keepers struggled to take them for walkies. And there was no dangerous traffic either, just a few small pedal-cars, and the odd electric tram purring by on the main road. Every-cat was acting as if this was all perfectly normal

21

– and no-cat was paying the least attention to two little school-kits as they trotted along. So Henry relaxed, and even began getting excited. Wow, he thought, I'm going shopping - for the first time in my life!

A bell tinged when MC pushed open the door of Mewly's Corner. Henry Wowler gazed around as the elderly shopkeeper shuffled slowly through from the back, thin of fur and grey round the whiskers, with a pair of gold-rimmed glasses perched on the end of her nose. Her shelves were laden with every flavour and type of tinned food, and biscuits, and big glass jars filled with savoury nibbles or sweets made from milk and catmint. He licked his lips over her cold-cabinets of fresh meat, fish, eggs, milk and cream, and the cooked meats behind the glass-fronted counter made him positively drool. How he'd love a piece of that roast chicken!

"What can I get you, young kit?" she asked.

"A packet of Goodpurr's Beefy-Rice Bix, please, Mrs Mewly," MC politely replied.

"*And* a bag of catnip-treats," hissed Henry, "please?"

"No, sorry." MC thrust his change deep into his pocket for safe-

22

keeping. "You'll understand when you see why I need the money."

Wishing the old cat goodbye, he led Henry out to the pet-shop next door, Oomans at 'Ome, and pointed to the window display.

"See? Now," he patted his pocket, "with next week's allowance, I can afford the bedroom set! And for my birthday, I've asked Mama and Papa to buy me *that*." He stood on tiptoe, nose and forepaws pressed to the glass. "Look, near the back... the big Deluxe Family Hutch. It's got an extra floor with three rooms, so they can have a proper kitchen, and a bedroom and nursery for Baby."

Beside him, Henry peered in at everything an Ooman-keeper could possibly want, from simple one-room hutches to luxury multi-storeys, ready-made furnishings, food, clothes, and accessories for Oomans of all ages – plus all the 'How To' books, tools, and materials for making and doing-it-yourself.

"Wow," he said faintly. The bedroom kit MC wanted had so many small wooden parts, fabric shapes and bags of stuffing, that he couldn't imagine what he'd do with them – except perhaps knock them one by one off a table for the fun of seeing them fall. "It looks very complicated."

"Oh, you just follow the instructions," said MC. "It's not hard. Although I don't sew very well, so Tabbi and Mama will make the mattress and bedclothes."

Just then the shop door burst open and the shopkeeper, a fat round grey tom in a brown overall, burst out shouting crossly,

"Oi! You! Scat! Get your mucky paws off my window! And stop wiping your nose on it – or I'll wipe it for you, in a way you won't like."

He made a grab for MC's tail, waving through the hole in the back of his shorts.

Quick as lightning MC sprang away and whipped it out of reach. "Oops – sorry, Mr Catwright," he said. "Let's go, Henry. I'll race you!"

Clutching his box of biscuits tightly, he sprinted away.

"Good boy." Mama-cat ruffled MC's head when they arrived back with five minutes to spare. "You've earned that change!

'Now, run along and finish your chores before dinner, then you can play with the Brights until bedtime."

"I hate it when she does that." MC smoothed his fur as they went through to the dining room. "Especially in front of guests! Because you *are* staying, aren't you? There'll be plenty, and Mama and Papa won't notice."

"Won't they? Why not? Why can't they see me?"

"Most grown-ups can't." To Henry's surprise, MC took a white cloth from the dresser drawer, spread it over the table and began laying plates. "But the longer you stay, the more solid you'll become until everyone can see you. Then we'll be twin brothers, and no-one will remember that you weren't always here."

He took some silver fish knives from a drawer. "So you really should join us. We always have salmon in cream sauce on Fridays-"

"Mm." Henry Wowler licked his lips. It sounded better than his usual tinned cat-food.

"-and catnip custard for pudding. It's very good."

"Mm-*mm*." Henry's whiskers drooped as MC laid cutlery by each china plate. "Oh – but I don't know how to eat with those things."

"You could easily learn." Waggling his forepaw, MC gave Henry a meaningful look.

Henry looked at the Mirror-cat's paw. He lifted his own paw. His eyes went wide and black. Just like MC's, it had changed! His toes didn't look like little pink beans now. No, they'd stretched out into little pink sausages – and he could wiggle them, just like Ooman fingers!

"But you can have a dish on the floor if you'd rather," MC went on, "and after dinner we can watch Tabbi feeding the baby. So do stay, Henry – it'll be fun."

Henry nodded. Yes, he thought, then we'll curl up in your blue bed, and have milk and biscuits for breakfast tomorrow, then feed the pets, and go to school, and I'll learn to do the things that two-legged cats do on This Side with fingers and thumbs... and very soon I'll forget all about my real home, and that I was ever a real four-legged cat... or was I? Living with big Oomans, and never wearing a collar or having to do chores, or schoolwork, or grow up and get a job... did I only dream those things? Is *this* my real home - here, with MC? He shook his head, trying to clear the confusion.

"What do you mean - *are* you staying for dinner, or aren't you?" asked MC. "Henry?"

A faint echo sounded in the distance. "Henry? Henry Wowler?"

Henry felt a tug in his heart. His mind's eye saw a familiar dining room with his own special mat, set with his own food and water bowls, and his own Oomans to fill them. He imagined the voice calling on, growing sadder by the day if he didn't appear. Suddenly he didn't care if that cat-life was only a dream – he was aching to get back there.

The tugging sensation grew stronger. Overflowing from his heart, filling him from the tips of his ears to the tip of his tail, it dragged him backwards, out through the hall, up the stairs, across into the big bedroom and over to the wardrobe. His school uniform peeled off in white, red and grey flakes as he went, then melted away into nothing.

The voice cried again, loud and clear. "Henry! Henry Wowler! Where are you?"

Dropping down onto all fours, Henry shut his eyes instinctively. With a final tug and a faint sucking sound, he found himself sitting on the bedroom carpet, blinking at the wardrobe's mirrored door.

He inspected a forepaw – back to pink beans. He was home.

"Henry Wowler? Oh, *there* you are," said a voice from the doorway, "admiring yourself again! Well, your tea's ready now – come and get it."

Henry sat a moment longer looking at the Mirror-cat, looking back at him. "Sorry I couldn't stay," he whispered. "Thanks for asking, though, and for showing me your pets and everything. It was very interesting to visit, but I don't think I'd like to live there. No offence."

"None taken. See you soon, Henry?"

"See you soon, MC."

Then, with his tail in the air, licking his lips at the prospect of cat-food, Henry Wowler followed his Ooman downstairs.

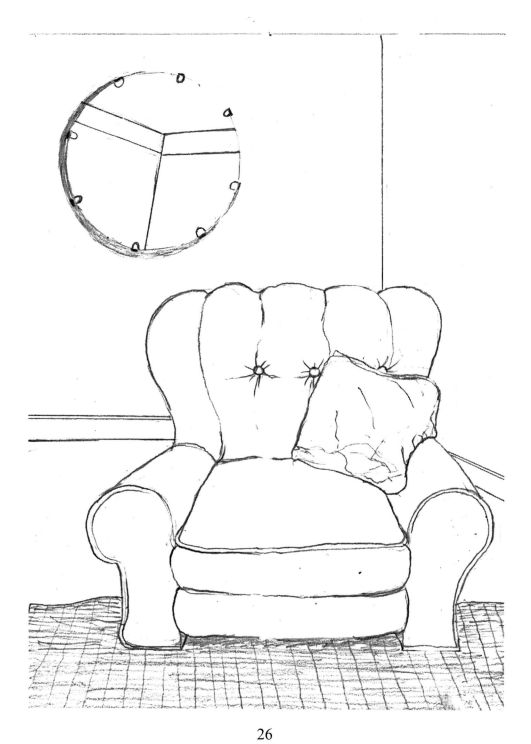

Chapter 3: Cat on the Wall

The living room mirror hung high and round on the wall, like a full moon or a blank eye, reflecting only the ceiling.

Henry Wowler thought it was the most boring mirror in the house. He could find MC in all the rest - even in the bathroom, if he stood on the sink – but never in this one. Prowling round on the carpet below, he gazed up at it from all sides. As usual, he couldn't see the Mirror-cat. And as usual, this made him very curious. Was there a room beneath that Other ceiling? What was it like? Was MC in there at this very moment, searching for him? Determined to find out, Henry jumped onto the nearest armchair, climbed up the armrest, and stood on the back. The mirror now showed him the upper wall and a corner of the door... but still no cat.

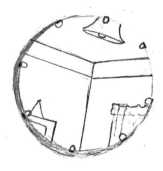

So he tried calling. "Hello? MC?"

Straining his ears, he heard a faint reply. "Hello? Henry?"

Encouraged, he sat up high on his haunches, craning his neck. The Mirror-cat's face popped into view – then popped out as the cushion squashed under his weight and made him wobble.

Regaining his balance, he sat up again. "Hello, MC! I'm glad I found you at last. What's it like over there? Is it good?"

"Better than good," said MC. "For some cats it's heaven."

"Wow! I'd like to see that." Henry's face fell. "But how do I get through? I can't get near this mirror."

"You have to make a leap of faith," said MC. "Just shut your eyes - and be sure to *keep* them shut until you land. That's very important."

Henry hesitated. No cat likes jumping blind. But if that was the only way... He stepped onto the top of the arm, which was harder than the cushion and would give a better take-off. In the mirror, he could just see the tips of MC's ears, bobbing and weaving as he adjusted his balance. He measured the distance – quite a long way. He waggled his bottom and shifted his paws. Taking a deep breath, he tensed every muscle and closed his eyes. A second later he opened them again, checked his aim at the centre of the mirror, and drew another deep breath. Then squeezing his eyes tightly shut, Henry thrust hard with his hind legs and leapt into space.

At the last possible moment, he panicked. His eyes snapped open. He saw MC flying towards him, desperately trying to brake in mid-air with his forepaws. Then a split-second later-

CRASH!

The mirror rattled against the wall, but luckily didn't break.

Henry Wowler dropped to the floor, landing neatly on his feet. Luckily, he didn't break either, although he and the Mirror-cat had smacked their faces together pretty hard.

"Ow." He rubbed his nose with a paw, imagining MC on the Other Side, doing the same. "That hurt."

So, what should he do now? Forget it – or try again? Henry thought for a moment, shook himself, then climbed back up the chair.

The Mirror-cat looked at him sternly. "Let's call that a practice jump, shall we? And it would've been a good one – if only you'd *kept your eyes shut*."

"Er, yes," said Henry. "Sorry, MC. I'll do it right this time."

He shifted and waggled into position again, screwed his eyes tight, held his breath, then launched himself at the mirror.

A second later, his paws struck the back of an armchair. Half-jumping, half-falling onto its seat, Henry opened his eyes. He found himself standing next to the Mirror-cat, who gave him a friendly head-butt.

"Well done! And now the hard part's over, we can enjoy ourselves."

Henry Wowler stared round, lost for words. The Other room was decorated like the one he'd just left, with the same armchair and carpet – but everything else was very different.

This carpet, littered with all sorts of wonderful toys, didn't stop at the walls but continued part way up them, all tufted and threadbare in places as if scratched by many claws. Above it, the walls were covered in photos of pedigree cats, displays of colourful rosettes, and glass-fronted cabinets of shining silver trophies. Instead of Ooman furniture, a big climbing frame stood in the middle of the room, surrounded by a long, snaking play-tunnel. In one corner was a tall scratching post with fluffy balls, jingly bells and feathers dangling from it, and opposite, a tower-block of six snug nests, each with its own porthole and balcony, and a wooden ladder giving access to them all.

"Ahem. Excuse me?" Henry looked down. What he'd taken for a round white fluffy cushion opened one turquoise eye and glared at him. "*Would* you mind not standing on my tail? Thank you *so* much."

"Oops – sorry." He moved a paw. "I didn't realise- I thought you were- um, never mind. Sorry."

"Apology accepted." The cushion stood up and arched its back. A pink mouth opened in a wide yawn. Then it shook long, spotless snowy fur back into place, sat down, and gave a long, unblinking look from Henry to the Mirror-cat.

"You again," it said to MC, "*and* you've brought company. Well, kindly vacate my throne, the pair of you. I don't want to catch your fleas."

"I haven't got fleas!" Henry protested, but he and MC jumped down anyway. "And I've had my injections, so you won't catch *anything* nasty from me."

"Hmm." The white cat thought for a moment. "In that case, I shall permit you to visit my court." She drew herself up. "The court, that is, of the Champion and Mother of Champions, Queen Snowberry Moonbeam Persian Beauty the Fourth, Best of Breed three years running. Which is *quite* an achievement and makes me *very* important and worth an awful lot of money. So you may kiss my paw, common cat."

"What?" spluttered Henry.

"Humour her," hissed MC, touching his nose to the outstretched forepaw. "Like this."

As Henry reluctantly obeyed, another magnificent long-haired cat came bounding towards them. "Hey, Queenie!" it cried.

The Persian winced. "Queen Snowberry, *if* you please."

"Don't keep the visitors all to yourself!" the other breezed on. "Hi, MC! Hi, stranger! You must be MC's twin - pleased to meetcha! I'm Stevie-"

"Ugh." Queenie shuddered. "I hate pet-names! Her Ladyship is *properly* called Stefelia Splendidfur Atlantic Glory."

"-and I'm a Maine Coon, from the US of A," Stevie finished, cocking her head at Henry Wowler. "What're *you*?"

Henry felt too stunned reply. He'd long prided himself on being the biggest cat on the block, so it was a shock to meet someone who dwarfed him – let alone this gorgeous lady-cat with her long, streaky golden-brown fur and huge amber eyes.

"Me? Oh, I, well," he floundered, "I'm, um, a-"

"Domestic shorthair," MC put in helpfully.

"Yes!" Henry shot him a grateful look. "What he said. That's us – domestic shorthairs."

A slim, elegant cat wandered over. Her creamy coat looked as if it had been dusted with cocoa, and her head, legs and tail dipped in dark chocolate.

"Eeuw," she said, looking down her long nose with slightly crossed sapphire-blue eyes. "*Moggies.*"

Stevie flicked her tail in disapproval. "Ah, c'mon, Dancy-"

"Lady Cappucino Temple-dancer Pride of Siam," muttered Queenie.

"-don't be rude to our guests." She almost knocked Henry flat with a friendly head-butt. "*I* think these twins are real cute-"

"Aye, for *Felis domesticus* they're no' bad." A pretty little tabby with an oddly round, kitten-like head, came up and touched noses. "Hello, lads. I'm Tammy."

"Lady Tam O'Shanter Glenmorangie MacTab of Perth." Queenie sighed.

"Wow-ow!" Henry gasped. "What's wrong with your ears?"

"My ears?" Tammy blinked in surprise. "Nothing, laddie – they're my best feature."

"But they're all scrunched up!"

A black cat with a strange stubby tail overheard and rolled her orange eyes. "Yes - she's a Scottish Fold! They're meant to be like that. Don't you commoners know *anything*?"

"Um- well, I know cats are meant to have tails," said Henry, rather stung by her tone.

"Not if they're a bobcat, or a lynx – or a Manx Supreme Champion and Isle of Man Cat of the Year," she retorted smugly.

Queenie nodded. "Yes, frankly, I'm surprised that even *you* haven't heard of Lady Morna Coalstar Bobblebott -"

"Or Bobbie, to her friends." A face looked down from the topmost balcony, bat-eared, bald and deeply wrinkled. Then an equally bald, skinny body

appeared, dressed in a pink woollen sweater with a white collar and cuffs. Henry thought it was the strangest creature he'd ever seen – even stranger than giant mice or miniature Oomans! Jumping nimbly down, she approached the group with her bony tail held high and looked straight at Henry Wowler.

"Before you ask, I am a Sphynx," she announced proudly. "No, I'm not old, I'm not ill, and it hasn't dropped out. Yes, actually, I *do* have fur, it's just very, very short. No, I *don't* envy your coat. I like wearing pretty clothes, and staying cool in summer, and not having to sick up hair-balls. And I *like* the name Skin. That's what everybody calls me." She winked at Queenie. "Well, nearly everybody."

"One does *try* to maintain fitting standards, Lady Skandria Desert-Lotus," Queenie said severely. "And now we're all assembled, ladies, let us hold court. You guests may sit at my feet," she added graciously to Henry and the Mirror-cat.

The other five formed a half-circle in front of the throne, their front paws together and tails, (all except Bobbie, of course), neatly curled round to cover their toes. With their bright eyes, glossy coats, (all except Skin, of course), and identical gold pendant collars, they were the six most glamorous, exotic cats Henry Wowler had ever imagined. Even the Sphynx had a peculiar grace, he thought, wondering if *he* looked like that under his fur, and hoping he'd never find out.

"Ahem." Queen Snowberry cleared her throat. "We have a rare treat today, ladies: two guests to entertain us!" She nodded at Henry. "May I present MC's brother, who will now introduce himself to us."

"Er, yes. Hello. I'm-" Henry paused. Plain Henry Wowler didn't sound much compared to their pedigree names, so he decided to dress it up a little. "I'm the Wowler," he said, sticking out his white chest. "Henry Wowler Gingerson the First, Dread of Night and expert rodent-slayer."

"Well, Dreaded Knight," said Queenie, "my ladies and I bid you welcome-"

"Rodent slayer?" Stevie broke in. "You mean you kill rats and mice? Wow! A hunter!" Her eyes lit up. "That's wild! Say, Henry Wowler, does that mean you're *feral*? Like what they call an *alley cat*?"

"No! At least, I do hang around in alleys sometimes," said Henry. "But I don't live in one. I've got a proper home with Oomans, and a microchip and everything."

Dancy squinted down her nose. "You haven't got a collar."

33

"No," Henry replied, "I always scratch them off. I don't like them, they make my neck itch."

MC nodded. "Mine, too."

"And your Oomans allow this?" Dancy stared in horror. "How dreadful! One can't tell from looking that you're not a- a- a *stray!*"

Henry shrugged. "Don't care. *I* know I'm not."

"Ooh," said little Tammy, "d'ye mean you go oot an' aboot, wi'oot a collar – *all by yersel'*? Ooh!" She looked at him appealingly with big, soft dark eyes. "Will you no' tell us about it, laddie? Please?"

"Yeah!" Stevie cried. "Tell us, Henry-"

"*Ahem.*" Queen Snowberry interrupted. "Ladies, ladies, please! Let our guests enjoy some hospitality first.

'As I was saying – welcome, MC and Henry Wowler! You'll find everyone here is *extremely* well-bred – not that you can always tell from their manners," she added, with a pointed look at Stevie. "*And* we're extremely successful." She waved a regal paw round at the prizes and pictures of prize-winning cats. "As you can see."

"Which makes us all very important," put in Bobbie.

"And worth an awful lot of money," said Dancy.

"And some of us are real famous," said Stevie. "Me, I'm the Face of TastyBix!" Bounding over to a large red furry ball, she jumped onto it and, taking tiny steps with all four paws, began rolling it around. "Good, huh? It gets better!" She stood on her hind legs and started to sing. "TastyBix, oh, TastyBix - hey, Skin! Toss me one!"

Pouncing on a pear-shaped plastic toy, the Sphynx batted it until a small biscuit fell out of a hole near the top. "Get ready," she cried, and picked it up in her teeth.

"Yee-haw! TastyBix, whoa TastyBix, cats'll do most anything, for a taste of TastyBix," sang Stevie. "Now!"

With a flick of her neck, Skin threw the biscuit.

Still expertly controlling the ball, Stevie snapped it out of the air. "Ta-da! See," she exclaimed happily, "I still got it!"

Henry Wowler gasped. "I know that song! And I've seen you do that trick before, ever so many times, on that moving-picture thing my Oomans watch! You look even better in the fur."

"Why, thank you!" Stevie and Skin returned to the circle. "Yeah, it sure was fun making that commercial. It got lots of prime-time viewing – and got me into the movies! I'm training now for my first starring-"

"Yes, well," Queen Snowberry cut her off, "we've all been on the screen at some time, Lady Stefelia-"

"And in the press, when we win things," put in Dancy. "Which is quite often, because we're all so perfect."

"Aye, so we do lots o' modelling, too." Tammy posed, arching her neck. "My face has graced many a tin o' Scottish shortbread."

"And I was the centrefold in last June's Manx Fanciers Monthly," said Bobbie.

"While my portraits have appeared on numerous calendars," said Queenie, "and my youngest daughters recently sat for a chocolate-box lid – a luxury assortment, naturally."

Skin sniffed. "Fashion favours the fluffy – as usual! Not that I'm exactly unknown in the show-business, I might add."

Queen Snowberry nodded. "That's why we have only the best here. We need do nothing for ourselves - Oomans wait on us paw and paw. We receive daily grooming and teeth-cleaning," she flashed gleaming fangs, "and a weekly bath-"

Henry Wowler gasped. "A bath? What, in water?"

"Mmm," she purred, "all nice and warm and bubbly."

"Then a blow-dry and fur-styling." Stevie nudged Skin. "For most of us, anyhow."

"And monthly check-ups from our private doctor, and all the latest toys for our amusement," Queenie went on, "and, of course, only the finest of foods.

'Speaking of which, would you care for something to eat? We had steak tartare for lunch, and there's plenty left."

"Wow!" Henry had never heard of steak tartare, but it sounded good. "Yes, please!"

Queenie leapt down from her throne. "Then come this way."

They followed her to a cat-flap in the corner, which lifted as Queenie drew near. "Collar activated," she said over her shoulder. Henry Wowler, who had to open his own flap with his nose, felt jealous. "Quick, before it shuts on you."

Henry and MC hurried through after her into a narrow conservatory running almost the length of the small garden. Its front was made largely of glass, set on top of a low brick wall, with long, cushioned window-seats on either side of a central door (which was propped open). Its back wall was made of brick, with various pegs and projections sticking out, and six roosting-shelves set at different heights.

For some reason Henry Wowler was reminded of the Bright family's hutch, but before he could work out exactly why, Queenie spoke again.

"Luxuriously appointed for taking the air, as you see. The, er, conveniences are down at the far end." She nodded towards six domed plastic litter-boxes. "Should the need arise, feel free to use any one, they're all very private. Opposite the door you'll find a biscuit dispenser – do help yourselves – and a spring-water drinking-fountain.

'Then up above you'll see our withdrawing quarters, should you care for a nap-"

Henry looked. On top of a big wooden bench he saw six smart wicker travelling baskets lined with fleecy cushions, each with a polished brass name-plate on its open door. Then he looked down on the floor underneath, which was far more interesting...

"-and our dining area below." Queenie finished, nodding at a row of white china bowls, each marked with a pet-name in gold letters. "If we'd known guests were coming, we would've saved more – but if you're still hungry when you've finished, you can fill up on TastyBix."

"Wow!" said Henry. "Thanks!"

Greedily, he and MC lapped up every delicious scrap of raw minced steak and beaten egg until all six bowls were shining clean. Then they helped themselves to a few biscuits from the dispenser, and washed them down with cool, refreshing water.

Afterwards, they sat on the doorstep washing their whiskers and looking out into the garden, which was completely different to Henry's own, apart from its shape and size. For a start, it was very tidy, and had no greenhouse, or shed, or flowerbeds, or log-piles for mice to hide in, or bushes and trees for birds to perch on. A broad, smooth, reddish path ran all the way past the conservatory, in front of the patio doors, and on round the side of the house. The rest of the space was taken up by a playground of bright green grass, complete with swings, a roundabout, a slide and a tunnel, all cat-sized, and three lawn sculptures built of concrete blocks and rings to climb on and run through. The only plant was a pot of long grass, and all around, instead of a hawthorn

hedge full of twittering sparrows, there was a solid brick wall topped with stout wire-mesh fencing.

Stevie trotted through the cat-flap to join them. "Whatcha think - pretty neat, huh?"

"Er, yes," said Henry, "very tidy. And I never knew there were so many great things for cats! I haven't got anything like this at home."

"Yeah, the Oomans sure make fun for us here. D'you guys wanna play?" Stevie's long fluffy tail whipped from side to side. "Yeah, c'mon, let's do the circuit! I'll race you!"

Without waiting for a reply, she ran up three steps onto the wooden bench, leapt from it to the first shelf, then set off for the next along the various paw-holds sticking out from the wall.

Henry and MC looked at each other. Next second, they gave chase, jumping and climbing after Stevie, all the way to the highest shelf in the farthest corner, then back to the middle by a different route, down onto the floor and out into the playground.

There, Stevie took a flying leap onto the roundabout, spun it a half-circle, leapt off again, snaked through, up and over the three sculptures in turn, ran up the slide steps and threw herself headlong down it, dashed through the tunnel, and finished by jumping onto a swing-seat, looking pleased with herself as she swung gently back and forth, waiting for the boys to catch up.

A few moments later, Henry Wowler panted up, and leapt – much too fast - at the neighbouring swing. It promptly tipped over. He turned a somersault and landed on his back with his paws in the air, feeling very silly – especially because the whole court had by now wandered out to watch their play.

He sat up and shook himself. Luckily, he wasn't hurt – the odd-feeling grass had broken his fall. Looking down, he treadled his forepaws and felt it. His face grew puzzled. Then he bent down to sniff.

"Uh- what? This isn't real grass!" he exclaimed.

"*Real* grass? With all mud and slimy worms in it? Eeuw!" said Bobbie. "Of course not! We might get soiled."

"Eeuw!" chorused the rest.

"Or pick up ticks and fleas." Dancy shuddered.

"Quite," said Queenie. "*We* like our grass in a pot, so we can have the odd nibble without getting dirty. And our path's made of a special gravel the rain soaks straight through, instead of making puddles – then it dries really fast so we don't wet our paws and catch cold. And we don't like trees full of stingy-bitey creepy-crawlies, either-"

"Eeuw," the other cats chorused again.

"Or *birds*," Bobbie said in disgust, as a greyish-white splat landed on the path beside her. "Eeuw," she moved away, "we don't want to encourage *those* filthy creatures. Not that they can get in, thank goodness."

Henry Wowler went suddenly cold in the tummy. The pigeon which had just dropped the splat was perched overhead, on wire netting that stretched from the conservatory roof to join up with the top of the fence. He gazed round in growing dismay. He'd been enjoying himself too much to notice that the garden was completely enclosed... and that all the doors and conservatory windows were covered outside with thick metal bars. *That* was why it reminded him of the Brights' hutch – it was nothing but a big fancy cage!

"Wow-oo," he wailed. "We're shut in!"

Queen Snowberry shook her head. "No, everything else is shut *out*. Everything dangerous and nasty. So don't worry, Henry Wowler. We're perfectly safe here, and very well guarded-"

"Because we're all very important," said Dancy.

"An' worth awfu' lots o' money," added Tammy.

Henry's eyes swivelled frantically. "But isn't there a flap? Can't you go out?"

"We *are* out," said Queenie.

"No," said Henry, "I mean *outside* out."

"Oh, yes," said Skin. "When we go in our baskets to shows and suchlike. Then we travel- oh, all over the place. Long ways away, in the car. I've even flown in aeroplanes."

"Wow." Henry, who never went further by car than a mile to the vet, (and was scared stiff every time), thought Skin must be very brave. "But I meant out there, actually." He pointed with his nose. "In the woods."

"Out *there?*" Bobbie gasped. "Oh, no! It's not safe! We'd be cat-napped!"

"Held to ransom!" cried Tammy.

"Or killed by jealous rivals!" Dancy shivered. "I wouldn't dream of setting a paw out *there-*"

"I would," Stevie murmured.

"-no, Outside's too great a risk for cats like us. After all, we're-"

"Very important and worth an awful lot of money," sighed Henry Wowler. "Yes, so you said. Well, I'm glad I'm not. It means I can do what I want, and go where I want, whenever I want."

Stevie sighed. "I'd sure like to hear about your life, Henry Wowler... you know, where you go, and what you get up to and all."

Tammy nodded. "Aye – will you no' tell us now? Please?"

"Yes, I must admit I'm curious," said Queenie. "*I'd* like to hear your story too, Dreaded Knight."

Henry felt that the least he could do was to entertain such kind hostesses. "Alright." He thought for a moment. "Well, it's very different where I come from-"

"Excuse me- where is that, exactly?" asked Skin.

"Er- over there," Henry waved a paw towards the house. "From the Other Side."

"So you live next door?" said Stevie. "That's nice - hi, neighbour!"

"Er- hi," he replied. "And I might only be a common cat, but my Oomans still care for me well. I get tasty food – not fancy, but plenty – for breakfast and dinner, and the odd treat in between.

'Mostly I sleep in the day, or go out in the garden. It's got real grass, and soil, and plants, and it's all open so anything can come in.

Birds, squirrels, and," Henry laid his ears back, "other cats. Then I shout at them to go away, and if they don't go, I hit them. Like this." He sat up on his haunches and struck out with his forepaws. "Biff! Pow!"

MC nodded solemnly. "He does, you know."

"Ooh!" the lady-cats chorused.

"Then later, my Oomans come home," Henry went on, "and we eat, and afterwards I let them cuddle me while they watch the moving picture. And at bedtime, they go upstairs to sleep and I go out."

"At night?" said Skin, her eyes wide with wonder. "In the dark? Without a coat? Even if," she shivered at the thought, "it's cold and rainy?"

"Well," Henry admitted, "then sometimes I just look out of the window. I usually go out though, I know lots of places to shelter. And if I get really wet, I shout for an Ooman to come down and dry me."

"Ooh," Dancy said enviously. "Night... I'd love to go outdoors at night. We only ever see it through the bars."

"Yes, for our own protection," said Queenie. "You know night's often the time when bad Oomans try to steal important cats who are worth an awful lot of money, like us." She turned to Henry Wowler. "But I don't suppose being stolen is something *you* have to worry about." (This was rather rude of her, but Henry's tale was starting to make Queen Snowberry feel so strange and uncomfortable and restless that she quite forgot her manners).

Luckily, he misunderstood. "No, at night I can hear Oomans coming a mile off. I just hide until they've gone past. So they can't steal me - they never even know I'm there."

"Hmm," said Tammy. "An' cats are meant to go oot at night, aren't we? That's why we see so well in the dark."

Henry nodded. "It's the best time for hunting – and there's nothing to beat a good mouse hunt."

"How d'you do it?" Stevie asked breathlessly. "How d'you catch the little critters?"

"Just sniff out where they go, wait there quietly, and when they come, pow! I pounce." Henry demonstrated.

"Ooh!" chorused the ladies.

"It's quite simple, really," he said modestly. "Mice aren't very clever. But I have to be careful not to kill them straight away. I like it best

41

when they try to run, so I can keep catching them over and over."

"Ooh. Then what?" said Tammy, wide-eyed.

"I take them home to play with in the kitchen. Sometimes they escape - but usually they die, and that's when I eat them." He purred at the memory. "Mm, those scrunchy little bones! Baby rabbits are even yummier, but I don't often find them – usually the foxes beat me to it."

"F-f-foxes?" quavered Skin. "R-real wild ones?"

"Oh, yes. But they don't bother me." Henry curled his lip. "They're just orange dogs with big tails, and they don't like things that fight back. The owls hunt at night, too – great big birds with big staring eyes." He glanced at Tammy. "Look a bit like you in the face."

"Ooh er." Dancy glanced nervously through the fence. "I think I'd just stay in the garden, then. The woods sound too dangerous-"

"You mean exciting!" cried Stevie. "I bet there ain't a fox or a owl alive we couldn't whip in a fair fight - huh, Henry Wowler?" Her voice turned yowly. "Ow-ooo-ow! And I wanna go see! *I* wanna go out at night!"

"Ow-ooo-ow," Tammy joined in plaintively, "me too!"

Their noise set off Bobbie, Dancy and Skin. "Mee-oow-ow!" they all cried. "Me-out! Me-out! ME-OUT!"

Queen Snowberry's control broke. "MEEEE-OW-OO-OW!" She threw herself at the fence and clung to the mesh with all her claws. "MEEEE-OUT-TOOOO!"

Suddenly, through their racket, Henry Wowler heard the back door open, then the thud of heavy footsteps, and a voice.

"My precious girls! What's wrong? Stop that caterwauling! I do hope you're not fighting." A very round She-Ooman with tightly-curled grey hair, wearing a white overall and a tweed skirt, appeared on the path. Her tightly-pursed little mouth opened wide in an O of surprise. Then she screamed, at the top of her voice.

"Tomcat! Michael! Oh, *Michael!* Quick, bring the net! That horrible tom's in with the girls again!"

A very round, bald-headed Ooman in a white overall and tweed trousers appeared beside her, clutching a large landing net. "What? How? Where?"

"There!" She pointed a trembling finger. "No wonder the girls are going crazy! Quick, quick, catch it before it does something dreadful!"

Henry Wowler froze. What'll happen if I get caught here, he thought, panic-stricken. How will I ever get home?

Then MC yelled at him. "Run!"

With that, all eight cats scattered, yowling and racing madly round the garden in every direction, almost tripping up Michael as he lumbered behind, swinging his net.

"Come here," he panted, "you wretched stray! I swear- if I catch you- I'll take you straight to the vet's- and have you put down!"

Buttons pinged everywhere as his wife ripped off her overall and spread it out wide, blocking the path. "Chase it into the conservatory," she cried, "and I'll shut the door! You'll be able to corner it in there."

The conservatory! Yes, thought Henry. Although he was much faster than Michael, the net had a long handle – and as it swished past again, only just missing his tail, he called desperately to Stevie.

"Help! Go indoors!"

"Sure thing, Henry Wowler." She leapt away from Michael's clumsy feet and dived through the doorway. "Now what?"

"Open the flap!" gasped Henry, dashing in after her.

"Okay." Stevie bounded over to the cat-flap. It lifted. She dived through, closely followed by Henry and MC.

Muffled shrieks came from outside. "It's gone in the girls' room! With Stefelia! Quick, get back in the house! Stop it, before-"

Sprinting to Queenie's throne, Henry leapt to the top of the arm. "Sorry – must go," he gasped to Stevie. Then, hardly bothering to check his aim, he squeezed his eyes shut and flung himself at the mirror.

Moments later, he found himself lying with his paws in the air for the second time that day – he'd jumped so hard that he'd flown right over the back of his own armchair, bounced off the seat, and fallen to the floor. He stayed like that for a minute, getting his breath back. Then he climbed carefully up the arm and looked in the mirror.

"Phew! I'm glad you're safe," he said with relief when MC's face appeared. "What's happening over there?"

"Oh, the Oomans are tearing the house apart," MC said cheerfully. "They can't understand how we got in – or out again."

"Oh dear," said Henry. "I feel awful now. I didn't mean to upset anyone. And I never even said goodbye to the ladies. I'd like to come back and apologise, and say thanks for having me."

"Er- you may not be able to," said MC. "No mirror ever shows exactly the same reflection twice, you know. So you can't be sure what you might find here a second time."

"Oh, that's a shame." Henry's whiskers drooped. "Perhaps I'd better not try this way again."

"Perhaps not. But never mind - I'll say goodbye for you."

"Would you?" He cheered up. "Thanks, MC. And tell them I think their side's- er, pretty neat – but I don't fancy living there. No offence."

"None taken." The Mirror-cat winked. "See you around, Henry Wowler."

Henry winked back. "See you around, MC."

He jumped down onto the seat, and curled up like a round, plump, orange-and-white cushion. Then, tired out by all the excitement, Henry Wowler drifted off into some *very* strange dreams…

Chapter 4: Cat at Night

He dreamed of MC's little Oomans and their baby, driving about in a shoebox on wheels pulled by six white mice... of Skin, parading down a catwalk in a sparkly dress... of himself, grown enormous, trying to catch Michael in a net... and of Stevie, wearing a top hat, bowling around on her big red ball.

She called to him as she rolled past. "Hey, Henry!"

His paws twitched.

"Hey, Henry! Henry Wowler!"

He woke up, yawned, stretched, opened his eyes.

"Henry! Hey, Henry Wowler! Over here!"

He looked. He blinked. He looked again, and still saw the same thing: Stevie's face, poking out of the mirror as she clung to its edge with her front claws.

"Hey, Henry Wowler!" she cried happily. "Surprise! It's me!"

Henry shook his head. "I'm still dreaming," he muttered.

"Uh-uh," said Stevie. "You're awake. I saw you go, remember? So when the hoo-hah died down, I just copied what you did." She heaved with her forepaws. "So what went wrong? I'm kinda stuck here."

"Ah," said Henry. "You must've opened your eyes too soon."

"Oh? So if I shut them now, could I wriggle through? I really, really want to come hunting with you."

"Hmm." Henry considered. "I don't know. It might be better if you try again later. Much later, when all our Oomans are asleep."

Her eyes lit up. "Sure thing, Henry Wowler!"

"Great – see you tonight, then." His whiskers drooped. "Ah. Actually, I might not be able- no, wait! You can do tricks, can't you?"

Stevie nodded. "Sure can."

"Right, then." Henry explained his problem. "Could you do that?"

She nodded again. "Sure! So, it's a date. But what do I do now?"

Henry shrugged. "Shut your eyes and let go, I suppose."

Stevie closed her eyes and opened her paws. "Oh-" Her face suddenly disappeared. "-kay," he heard, very faintly, from the Other Side.

Henry Wowler was so excited he could hardly wait until darkness fell and his Oomans finally went to bed. He sat by the living room door for what felt like ages; prowled restlessly around the kitchen; went in and out through his cat-flap several times; then sat by the door again.

At last he heard a scrabbling sound, followed by a soft thud. His heart leapt. Then the door handle moved, and the door opened slightly. Henry pulled it ajar with his claws and squeezed through.

Stevie greeted him with a triumphant head-butt. "Hi, Henry Wowler! So, we got a hole through to next door! Who knew, huh?"

"It's not exactly a hole," he replied. "It's a mirror."

"A what?"

"A mirror. It shows you stuff. Get up and have a look."

Stevie sprang onto the back of the armchair and sat up on her haunches. "Hey!" she exclaimed. "Who's that? She looks just like me."

"Yes, she's your twin – like MC's mine."

"Wow! Cool." Stevie waved a paw at her Mirror-cat, who waved back. "Can she come with us?"

"Hmm." Henry shook his head. "I don't think so. It doesn't seem to work like that."

"Too bad. Ah, well – so long, sis!" She waved goodbye, then jumped down and headed for the kitchen. "Let's go, Henry. Show me Outside."

"Er- can you shut the door first? My Oomans will wonder what's happened if they come down and find it like that."

"No problemo." Stevie stood on her hind legs, pulled down the handle with her forepaws, then pushed the door closed. "But why? You told us you could go anywhere you wanted, any time."

Henry felt hot under his fur. "Um- because of the mice I bring in," he confessed. "The Oomans don't want me chasing them all round the house, so they make me stay in the kitchen at night. I don't really mind, though. I've got water and biscuits in here, and a nice comfy basket. Not that I use it very often." He went over to his cat-flap. "It's much more fun outdoors."

"Oh yeah – let's go Have An Adventure!" Stevie pushed past and dived through the flap.

Henry followed at a sensible speed and found her sitting on the path, gazing up at the twinkling stars.

"Awesome!" As she strained her nose high to sniff the air, a haunting cry rang out overhead. "Yow!" She crouched down. "What was *that*?"

"Just an owl," said Henry. "You probably won't see one-"

"Twit-twoo!" the unseen owl butted in. A distant reply came, "Twoo-hoo."

"-but you'll hear plenty."

"The night-birds?" Stevie shrugged. "Okay, cool. So now," following her nose, she padded away, "what all smells so fine back here?"

She prowled round the lawn and flower-beds, drank some water from the bird-bath, wriggled about in the big patch of catmint, and exclaimed in delight, "Wow! Your garden's much better than ours, Henry Wowler! I could stay here all night if I wasn't so wild to go hunting."

"Well, you could hunt here - I'll show you." He led Stevie to an open-fronted shed filled with neat stacks of logs. "What do you smell?"

She sniffed. "Wood, I guess. And- eeuw," her nose wrinkled, "something kinda fusty, like an old dirty litter-tray."

"Yes, that's Mouse. They nest at the back, where I can't reach them," Henry licked his lips, "until they come out to feed. But I know an even better spot, if you'd rather go out in the woods."

Stevie nodded eagerly.

"Good," he went on, "so remember the scent-"

"Eeuw! I couldn't forget if I tried!"

"-because that's what we'll be tracking."

"Can't wait!" She squeezed after him through the scrolls of the wrought-iron side gate, then stopped short. "Ee-*uw*." Her nose wrinkled again. "Now what's *that*?"

The familiar rank odour reached Henry. "Ah. That," he began, as a scruffy ginger tom strolled out of a bush, raised his tail, and sprayed on the lower leaves, "that's my dad."

The cat heard and glanced over. "Eh up, son." Then he spotted Stevie. His jaw dropped. "Me-*yow*! Who's your lady-friend?"

"That's your pa? Yay!" Stevie bounded away to bump noses. "Hi there! You must be Ginger - glad to meetcha! I'm Stevie."

"Oh yes?" Ginger cocked his head. "I know all the local kitties, but I ain't seen you before." He winked at her. "And I'd remember! So, where you from then, Stevie?"

Henry Wowler butted in before she could say anything about mirrors, or the Other Side – he didn't want to spend all night trying to explain it to Ginger. "Stevie's just visiting, dad. For a hunting trip. We're off mousing in the woods."

"Yeah – why not come along, Henry's pa? We could make like a real family outing."

"Sorry, lass, I can't. I'm already late for a date-" Ginger's ears pricked up as a loud caterwauling began in the next street. "An' that sounds like her complaining! Sorry, kits – must run." He slipped through the front gate, and with a farewell flick of his tail, vanished into the night.

"Whew! Your pa's some character," said Stevie, "and I guess you get used to the smell. Too bad he couldn't join us… but I'm raring to go!"

The gate bars were too narrow for them to go through like Ginger, so they jumped over it instead. Blinking up at the tall orange streetlight, Stevie exclaimed happily, "Wow! Look at me – Out At Night like a proper cat! So where are these mice, Henry Wowler?"

"Back here." He turned onto a narrow muddy lane between the houses, leading Stevie past the hedges of their gardens, away from the glowing street, into the darkness beyond.

All of a sudden, from the long grass and nettles, a long, rusty shape appeared. Henry stopped dead in his tracks.

"Whoa!" Stevie ran into him. "Oh, wow! 'Orange dog with big tail' - is that a fox?"

"Yes-s-s," Henry hissed, arching his back and glaring at it. "S-so fluff yourself up – be as big as you can."

"Sure thing!" Stevie rose tall on her hind legs, fuzzing out every strand of long fur.

"Hey, dog!" she snarled. "You looking for trouble? 'Cause you've found some - me an' the Dread of Night here."

The fox's tail drooped. "Oh, no. Not looking for trouble," it whined, pressing close to the hedge to slink by. "Just looking for scraps. I'll be on my way now. 'Scuse me...."

Watching it sprint for the street, Stevie returned to all fours. "Easy-peasy," she said, faintly smug.

"Yes, well," said Henry, secretly impressed, "I didn't expect any bother – your average fox prefers raiding dustbins to attacking big, dangerous things! And we'll be the biggest, most dangerous things out tonight. Well, probably. Just stay away from the Ooman path, and if a loose dog comes sniffing round, head straight here." He pointed with his nose to a gap between the thorny hedge and a fence made of old railway sleepers. "It's a shortcut into our back garden. Nothing can get at us there."

"Okay... scare off foxes, avoid Oomans, run from dogs, and remember the mouse-smell – eeuw! Got that." Stevie took a deep breath. "Ready to roll, Henry Wowler."

The muddy lane led to a long, narrow strip of woodland behind the back gardens of the houses, with a small stream running through it and open fields beyond. All kinds of creatures nested in its dense undergrowth, inside hollow trees, or burrowed into the banks of the stream – and just like the cats, many came out at night to hunt.

"WOW!" Stevie ducked as a small dark something swooped low overhead, chittering tiny, high-pitched squeaks. "Was that a *mouse*? It smelt kinda like one. But you never said they could *fly*!"

"Shush!" hissed Henry. "No, it was a bat. Which *is* a sort of flying mouse, I suppose-"

A voice from above cut in. "What's all this to-do? Oh, you-hoo again," it said grumpily to Henry. "And whoo's that with you? *Another* mouse-thief? Boo!"

"Who said that?" Stevie looked up. Her eyes opened wide. "Hey, a owl! Henry said you all look like my friend Tammy, and so you do! Except she hasn't got wings. Or a beak."

"I don't care a hoot." The owl coughed out a pellet to land at their feet. "Go home, you-hoo wretched creatures! Stop stealing my mice."

"They're not *your* mice," protested Henry. "They're anyone's."

"Anyone *wild*, not pets like you-hoo!" sniffed the owl. "*You* don't need to eat them. We do."

"Aw – c'mon, Owl," said Stevie. "I've never stolen or eaten a mouse in my life! But I'd sure like to tonight, this one time."

"Pooh." The owl glared. "Do-hoo as you like. You've already spoiled *my* hunting, so I'll leave you to-whit. To-whoo!"

It sailed off into the dark on silent wings.

"Oops," said Stevie. "Owls don't like us much, huh?"

"No," replied Henry, "they don't. But hunting's in *our* nature as well, so that's what we're jolly well going to do… unless we've scared all the mice away, making so much noise."

"Gee, I hope not! Oops," Stevie lowered her voice to a whisper, "sorry, Henry Wowler. I'll hush now."

With that, the cats set off creeping through the tall vegetation, their eyes wide and black, ears pricked, and whiskers alert. Soon they picked up a certain smell, faint at first but quickly growing stronger, until they reached a thick bramble patch in a small clearing, where it almost overpowered them.

"Stop," Henry hissed. "See that tunnel in the grass? It's a mouse-way, and they'll be coming and going along it all night for these berries. So we just sit quiet and wait for the next one – then pow! We pounce!" He demonstrated. "Just like that! Then you can eat it, or play with it – whatever you want."

"Okay," Stevie hissed back. She crouched low beside Henry in a tuft of long grass, her eyes fixed to the mouse-way's dark opening. "I hope we don't have to wait long. I'm already so excited I could pee."

Luckily, after just a few minutes, they smelled a fresh scent and heard rustling grass. A pointed, twitching nose appeared, followed by a pair of beady eyes. Then, very slowly, the whole head poked out, listening hard with its pale, rounded ears.

The cats held their breath.

The mouse looked at the brambles, sniffing their ripe, luscious scent. It badly wanted to eat them – so a few seconds later, it emerged.

"Pow!" Stevie leapt from hiding and slammed her right forepaw down hard on its tail. "Just like that, Henry Wowler! Look, look. I got it! Pretty good for a first-timer, huh?"

"Eek!" the mouse squeaked, scrabbling with all four sets of tiny claws, desperately trying to free itself, until Stevie bent low to watch. Then it froze.

"Oh." She patted the mouse gently with her left paw. It didn't move. "Did it just die?" She lifted her other paw from its tail. It still didn't move. "Yeah – died of fright, I guess," she said sadly.

"No!" Henry cried. "Don't let go! It's not dead, it's only pretending! It's hoping you'll get bored and go away."

"Oh. Okay." Stevie put her paw back. "Now what?"

"I'll show you," he said eagerly. "Bat it over here, I'll get it moving!"

"Um." She inspected it, hunched like a brown furry ping-pong ball. "Mice are real small, huh? *And* kinda cute. I don't want to hurt the li'l guy."

"Kill it quick, then, and eat it! Go on, it's a nice juicy one – you'll enjoy it."

"Um. I dunno." Stevie sniffed, doubtfully. Her nose wrinkled. Then to Henry's surprise, she stretched out her free paw, hooked the nearest fat bramble, and dropped it by the still nose.

The nose gave a very slight twitch.

"Aha! You *are* still alive, then! Go ahead, li'l guy - tuck in."

"*What?* What are you *doing*?" cried Henry. "You don't feed prey, you bite it! Kill it! Eat it!"

"Um… I don't think so." She released the tail. "There you go, li'l guy – you're free. Don't be scared, now. We won't hurtcha."

"We won't?"

"No, Henry Wowler," Stevie said firmly, "we won't.

The mouse sniffed at the fruit. Then, very slowly, it sat up.

"Aw." Very slowly, Stevie lowered her head and, very gently, bumped her nose on its tiny snout. "Hey, Mousie!" she whispered. "Take your gift now and run along home."

Very slowly, she backed away and sat down.

Amazed, the mouse looked from her to Henry Wowler. "Thanks," it squeaked. Then seizing the blackberry in its jaws, it vanished into the mouse-way in a single mighty leap.

Henry Wowler shook his head. "I can't believe you just did that," he sighed. "What a waste!"

"Not for me," said Stevie. "No, I caught a real live mouse, on my first try!" She preened her whiskers. "Which makes me a hunter. A *real* cat. And that's good enough for me. Anyhow, you said to 'do whatever you want.' So I did."

"Hmm." Henry wasn't impressed. "Well, there's no point hunting any more. So what do you want to do now?"

Stevie put back her head and yawned. "Make tracks, I guess. I feel kinda tired... I usually sleep nights. But can we go back a different way, please? I'd like see some more Great Outdoors before I head home."

"Of course. I know lots of ways, but I think you'll like this one best." Henry led her through the undergrowth, across a well-trodden Ooman path, and on down to follow the bank of the stream. Although they didn't meet any more creatures as they passed, they heard plenty - squeaking and rustling in the undergrowth, splashing in the water, and calling all around from near and far.

Proud of her new knowledge, Stevie exclaimed, "Owl!" whenever one hooted from the treetops, or, "Bat!" whenever one flitted past – although being unable to tell, she had to ask, "Dog or fox?" every time something barked from the gardens or fields. To Henry, used to prowling alone and in silence, this was rather wearing, so he felt mildly relieved when they at last reached his lane, trotted down to the shortcut and hopped through it into his garden.

"Wow-ee!" Stevie sat beside him on the path. "That was some night - thanks, Henry Wowler! I can't wait to tell the girls, they'll go wild."

"I enjoyed it, too," said Henry. "Your company, I mean. I'm not so sure about the hunting."

"Ah, c'mon." She barged his shoulder playfully, almost knocking him over. "That was the best bit! Anyhow," she stretched and yawned widely, "I'd love to stay and play a while longer, but I really should hit the hole-in-the-wall before the Oomans miss me."

They strolled slowly back to his cat-flap, where Henry stopped short in dismay. "Oh no!" he exclaimed. "Look at this."

Stevie peered in through the clear plastic. "Hey – who left the light on? It was dark when we left, wasn't it?"

"Yes," Henry said grimly. "Which means my She-Ooman got up early. She often does. And she'll be in the same room as the mirror."

"Oh-oh. So I have to get past her to get out? That's not good."

"Hmm. It might not matter," he replied thoughtfully. "She might not be able to see you. I don't know why, I don't understand mirror-worlds. MC does, though. I wish he was here now – he'd tell us what to do."

"Well, he isn't, so we'll have to come up with our own plan! Go see what your Ooman's doing, Henry Wowler. Maybe you can distract her while I sneak out."

"Good idea." Slowly, quietly, Henry nosed his cat-flap open. Slowly, quietly, he oozed through, holding it on the tip of his tail and closing it slowly and gently behind him, with only the softest of clicks.

He held his breath, but there was no cry of greeting from the living room, only the light of a lamp shining through its part-open door. On silent paws, Henry crept over and peeped in. Sure enough, she was in there under a blanket on the couch, a mug and a half-empty coffee-pot on the table beside her, and a book in her hand... but her eyes had closed, her glasses had slipped down her nose, her mouth hung slightly open – and as he watched, she began to snore.

Padding back to the cat-flap, he hissed, "We're safe! She's asleep."

Stevie crept in. "Whew - lucky break! So, I guess this is goodbye." She bumped noses with him. "Thanks again, Henry Wowler. I hope we have another adventure together real soon."

"Me too," said Henry. "Meanwhile, here's the plan: run and jump, straight up the armchair and through the mirror. She'll never know you were here." He paused, imagining Stevie's rear end stuck half way through the glass. "Just remember to shut your eyes tight till you land!"

"Sure," she whispered, taking up position in the doorway. "Run to chair, jump up back, shut eyes, jump at mirror, *keep 'em shut* - check.

Okay... this is it! So long, pal."

"Yes - 'bye for now, Stevie." He rubbed cheeks with her. "Ready?"

She wriggled her bottom and shifted her paws. "Uh-huh."

"Steady?"

Her whole body tensed. "Uh-huh."

"Then *go!*"

Without even a glance at his Ooman, Stevie crossed to the armchair in three strides, and jumped onto the back. There she paused for a split second to gather her balance. Then she leapt - and must have kept her eyes properly shut, because Henry's last glimpse of her was a fluffy tail-tip disappearing through the glass.

So, she'd made it home, as a fully-fledged mouser – of sorts. Henry stood for a moment, thinking about her, wishing that she could have stayed longer. Then he thought about an early breakfast, and his ginger tail rose in happy expectation.

Trotting into the living room with a loud, "Wow!" he realised that his Ooman had already woken.

"What? Where? Oh – hello, Henry Wowler." She propped herself up on one elbow, straightened her glasses, then peered over the back of the couch as if looking for something – or someone. Frowning, she untangled herself from the blanket and went to check behind the curtains, petting Henry as she passed. Then she searched the rest of the room, peering underneath and around the furniture.

Finally she stopped in front of the mirror and tapped the glass with her fingernail. "I could've sworn I was awake. But I can't have been," she said to her reflection. "I can't have seen- I must've dreamt- but she seemed so *real*."

"She *was*," replied Henry; but it came out as, "Miaow," and the She-Ooman didn't understand.

"Silly old Mummy-cat," she laughed, bending to fuss him. "Been watching too many TastyBix adverts, haven't I? And I bet you'd like some of those now, Henry Wowler."

Eagerly, Henry followed her into the kitchen. I wish I could explain about Stevie, he thought. Ah well... at least now I know that some Oomans *can* see Mirror-cats. So if I get any more visits from the Other Side, we'd better be very careful indeed – or who knows what might happen?

THE END

About the Hero:

Henry Wowler, Ginger's son (probably), was born in Wakefield, West Yorkshire, in August 2011. At eight weeks old he ran away from home and went wild in the woods for a fortnight. Then on one dark November night, he was found under a bush, lost, cold, hungry and crying for his mum, and brought home to live with two new Oomans.

He's never strayed far away since, or stayed out too long – he's much too fond of his creature comforts – and has become a popular feature on his She-Ooman's Facebook page, website and blog. As a big full-grown tom, Henry now works as a cupboard inspector, pest control officer, cat-flap guard and part-time lap-warmer. His hobbies include watching nature documentaries about polar bears or creatures hunting other creatures, (perhaps looking for tips on his favourite pastime).

Henry's favourite foods are chicken, steak and mice, but he'll make do with tinned cat food. He enjoys custard, but never drinks milk, and seldom plays with toys (apart from the odd catnip mouse) since he learnt how to catch the real thing. He loves eating, sleeping, being brushed, and having his big soft white tummy rubbed. His pet hates are noise, visitors, and being talked to or touched without permission.

Find out more on the **Henry Wowler** Facebook page!

About the Author:

Rae Andrew is the fiction pen-name of Helen Cox. After studying archaeology and conservation at university, Helen spent two decades working in the heritage profession as a museum antiquities conservator and consultant.

In 2005 she retired to Wakefield, moved in with her husband-to-be, and set up a new business, Herstory Writing & Interpretation. She has since published numerous articles for historical and local interest magazines, as well as self-publishing three non-fiction history books on the battles of Wakefield and Towton, and, as Rae Andrew, a tongue-in-cheek adult fantasy trilogy, *The Lay of Angor.* In between writing and acting as a cat-mattress, Helen has also worked as a freelance speaker, Wars of the Roses interpreter for schools, historical walk/tour guide, secular funeral and wedding celebrant, and more recently, as assistant to her professional gardener and smallholder husband.

Helen is currently working on *An Accidental Kitten*, the biography of Henry Wowler, and under her pen-name, a fully-revised second edition of the *Lay*, condensed into a single volume for re-release in French as *Chanson d'Angor.* She also has plenty of ideas for the further adventures of Henry and the Mirror-cats, so watch out for a sequel!

Find out more on **www.herstorywriting.com**

About the Artist:

Janet Flynn, BA Fine Arts, Post Grad (Slade), PGCE (Huds), set up her company, Flynn Fine Art, soon after finishing her creative training. FFA worked with Theatre and Arts organisations as well as Universities, Local Authorities, Prisons and Hospitals. Janet's roles within these organisations was to facilitate the delivery of arts related projects. The company ran successfully for nearly thirty years providing support for private individuals in the creation of exhibitions, as well as for local arts groups.

Throughout her career Janet continued her own practice as an artist, illustrator, ceramics and print maker, working in a wide range of styles and media. Her work has been exhibited nationally and internationally, and she is a respected and well-known figure in the arts community of Northern England.

In 2019, Janet moved with her husband to Syros in Greece to concentrate on her painting. *Henry Wowler & the Mirror-Cat* is her first – but hopefully not her last – foray into book illustration.

Acknowledgements:

This book would not have been possible without my husband Michael Doggett, who started off the whole adventure by finding a little lost Henry Wowler and bringing him home in the first place, then put up with the consequences – which all long-suffering cat-parents can imagine - for nine years and counting. Lately, said consequences have included an untidy, preoccupied wife, an untidy, dusty house, lots of hasty scratch dinners, and lots of alone time in bed while, gripped by the story, I sat up nights pounding the keyboard; so I'll be eternally grateful that he bore all this with patience, good humour, and an encouraging faith in the work.

To my good friend Janet Flynn I owe a lasting debt of gratitude for bringing the text to life with her superb illustrations. Not only do they capture Henry Wowler to perfection, they capture the surreal edge of the stories, and of the characters as I saw them in my mind's eye – a kindred spirit and great artistic talent.

I'm also deeply grateful to everyone who read and commented on the drafts, especially my cousin, art teacher and sculptor Sarah Peterson, for her support and constructive feedback.

And last but not least , I thank my beloved furry friend and lap-warmer, Henry Wowler, for the entertaining antics which inspired these stories (and often hindered my attempts to write them down). Above all, I thank him for simply being himself – a unique character, and an extremely fine cat.

Rae Andrew
August 2021

Other Herstory Publications:

Non-fiction by Helen Cox:

The Battle of Wakefield Revisited: a fresh perspective on Richard of York's final battle, December 1460

Walk Wakefield 1460: A Visitor Guide to Battle-Related Sites

Walk Towton 1461: A Visitor Guide to Battle-Related Sites (co-author Alan Stringer)

Fiction by Rae Andrew:

The Lay of Angor Book 1: Gondarlan
The Lay of Angor Book 2: Breath of Gaia
The Lay of Angor Book 3: Wolfsbane

Forthcoming:

An Accidental Kitten: the Tail of Henry Wowler
The Lay of Angor, revised single volume 2nd edition in English and French